SHADOW
SQUADRON

SNIPER SHIELD

WRITTEN BY
CARL BOWEN

ILLUSTRATED BY
WILSON TORTOSA

COLOURED BY
BENNY FUENTES

2012.241

AUTHORIZING

RAINTREE IS AN IMPRINT OF
CAPSTONE GLOBAL LIBRARY LIMITED,
A COMPANY INCORPORATED IN ENGLAND AND WALES HAVING ITS
REGISTERED OFFICE AT 7 PILGRIM STREET, LONDON, EC4V 6LB
REGISTERED COMPANY NUMBER: 6695582

WWW.RAINTREEPUBLISHERS.CO.UK
MYORDERS@RAINTREEPUBLISHERS.CO.UK

FIRST PUBLISHED BY STONE ARCH BOOKS © 2013
FIRST PUBLISHED IN THE UNITED KINGDOM IN 2014
THE MORAL RIGHTS OF THE PROPRIETOR HAVE BEEN ASSERTED

DESIGNED BY BRANN GARVEY

ISBN 978 1 406 26656 6 (PAPERBACK)
17 16 15 14 13
10 9 8 7 6 5 4 3 2 1

PRINTED AND BOUND IN CHINA BY LEO PAPER PRODUCTS LTD

BRITISH LIBRARY CATALOGUING IN PUBLICATION DATA
A FULL CATALOGUE RECORD FOR THIS BOOK IS AVAILABLE FROM THE
BRITISH LIBRARY

CONTENTS

ACCESS GRANTED

Z012.101

SHADOW SQUADRON DOSSIER

CROSS, RYAN

RANK: Lieutenant Commander
BRANCH: Navy SEAL
PSYCH PROFILE: Cross is the team leader of Shadow Squadron. He likes to be in control and insisted on hand-picking each member of his squad.

WALKER, ALONSO

RANK: Chief Petty Officer
BRANCH: Navy SEAL
PSYCH PROFILE: Walker is Shadow Squadron's second-in-command. His combat experience, scepticism, and distrustful nature make him a good counter-balance to Cross's command.

YAMASHITA, KIMIYO

RANK: Lieutenant
BRANCH: Army Ranger
PSYCH PROFILE: The team's sniper is an expert marksman and a true stoic. It seems his emotions are as steady as his trigger finger.

BRIGHTON, EDGAR

RANK: Staff Sergeant
BRANCH: Air Force Combat Controller
PSYCH PROFILE: The team's technician and close-quarters-combat specialist is popular with his squadmates but often irritates his commanding officers.

JANNATI, ARAM

4236.052

PHOTO NOT AVAILABLE

RANK: Second Lieutenant
BRANCH: Marine Special Ops Regiment
PSYCH PROFILE: Jannati is a talented linguist with extensive experience performing special ops in small teams.

SHEPHERD, MARK

1216.062

PHOTO NOT AVAILABLE

RANK: Lieutenant
BRANCH: Army (Green Beret)
PSYCH PROFILE: The heavy-weapons expert of the group, Shepherd's love of combat borders on unhealthy.

2019.681

MISSION BRIEFING

OPERATION

SNIPER SHIELD
1234

This will be a VIP protection mission, men. We'll be guarding a man named Heshem Shadid, an Iraqi politician. Fair warning: some of you may take issue with the fact that Shadid is a former terrorist. However, he's also a valuable asset to the war effort, and his former friends are none too pleased that Shadid has switched sides. They'll do anything to take him out. I expect you all to put aside your feelings and demonstrate what it means to be a soldier. Yamashita will be on overwatch with me. The rest of you will be co-ordinating with Shadid's men to safeguard him en route to his destination.

3245.98 ●●●

— Lieutenant Commander Ryan Cross

IRAQ

PRIMARY OBJECTIVES

- Meet with the VIP and his personal security force

- Prep a route and determine an overwatch position for transit

- Protect the VIP en route to his destination

SECONDARY OBJECTIVES

- Avoid open conflict with Iraqi insurgents

- Keep our presence covert

1932.789

0412.981

1624.054

9

INTEL

DECRYPTING
|||||||||| |||||||||||||| |||||||

12345

COM CHATTER

- AK-47 - Russian-made, cost-efficient gas-operated assault rifle

- M110 SNIPER RIFLE - an American-made, semi-automatic sniper rifle

- M4 CARBINE - short and light selective-fire assault rifle

- OVERWATCH - a small unit supporting another unit from a position where the terrain ahead can be seen

3245.98 ● ● ●

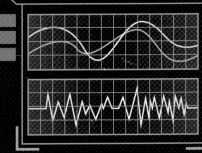

OVERWATCH

Shadow Squadron was in Iraq, and had been operating there for the past several weeks. Officially, the US-led war had been over for years, and the last of the American combat forces had withdrawn months ago. Iraq, however, was still a bed of chaos. Terrorist organizations and local militias continued to stir up endless problems for the newly elected government. The remaining internal threats were so severe that even some of the locals admitted they weren't ready to handle them on their own.

So they called on their American allies for help – namely, Shadow Squadron.

Lieutenant Commander Ryan Cross glanced up at the sun and shielded his eyes. The blistering heat in Nasiriyah, in south-eastern Iraq, was intense. The searing sun and extremely dry air were impossible to ignore. But in the midst of an operation, with death hiding around every corner or lurking in every shadow, there wasn't time for distractions. Mental lapses could prove to be fatal.

Fortunately, the men under Cross's command were some of the best-trained soldiers in the world. Members of Shadow Squadron were recruited from all branches of the American military, and were handpicked by Cross himself. The squad trained tirelessly. They had to be ready at a moment's notice for missions all over the world.

They were, quite literally, the elite of the elite. So when duty called, it took much more than extreme temperatures or physical discomfort to affect the team's focus.

For the most part, Shadow Squadron's assistance in Iraq had involved training local military forces, or providing protection for local VIPs who didn't yet trust their own soldiers. Occasionally, Cross and his men were given direct-action assignments such as live fire raids on hostile targets. Like today.

Acting on a tip from a trusted politician from the Dhi Qar Province, Cross's eight-man squad was tasked with an assault on an Al Qaeda insurgent cell.

The cell was currently holed up in an abandoned apartment complex in Nasiriyah. According to the tip, the cell was planning to sneak bombs into the Drainage Pump Station along the Euphrates River. Intel confirmed that the cell had been stockpiling explosives in their hideout for months. The Nasiriyah station was the largest in the Middle East. It was likely that the insurgents hoped to disable a vital public structure. Or to strike fear into the hearts of the locals.

Either way, Cross had decided that now was the time to act.

WHIR-WHIR-WHIR-WHIR!

Shadow Squadron's black Seahawk helicopter roared in low over the skyline. It briefly paused over the abandoned apartment building. Almost immediately, six members of Shadow Squadron fast-roped down onto the roof. The chopper then hopped over to another building across the street. There two more team members dropped in, including Kimiyo Yamashita, the team's sniper. These two would act as overwatch for the rest of the team, picking off any insurgents who tried to escape.

So far, the operation was proceeding smoothly. Cross and his second-in-command, Chief Petty Officer Alonso Walker, led the six-man squad down into the building. They made their way through the structure slowly, checking blind spots and covering each other's backs. They encountered no resistance – until they reached the ground floor. Cross and his men had caught the insurgents in the middle of lunch. To say they were caught unprepared would be an understatement.

Cross grinned, and then squeezed the trigger of his M4 carbine.

BANG!

Cross fired a single round into the ceiling as a warning shot. One of the Iraqis sprinted out of the room. The rest of the insurgents fell over themselves trying to surrender.

Cross motioned for Walker and Sergeant Mark Shepherd to join him in pursuit of the fleeing hostile. The remaining three members of Shadow Squadron stayed behind to secure the non-combatants.

Cross chased the fleeing insurgent down a corridor and around a corner. Suddenly, the insurgent popped out from a half-open door with an AK-47 in his hand.

RAT-TAT-TAT-TAT-TAT!

RAT-TAT-TAT-TAT-TAT!

RAT-TAT-TAT-TAT-TAT!

The Iraqi sprayed bullets wildly at Cross and his men.

Ducking out of harm's way just in time, Cross reached around the corner with his rifle to throw out suppressing fire. The spray forced the Iraqi back into his hole, and also bought enough time for Walker and Shepherd to rush around the corner and get into cover positions down the corridor.

When the insurgent stuck his head out to see once again, he was surprised to see all three Americans open fire. Chief Walker managed to hit the Iraqi in the side by firing straight through the cheap drywall beside the door frame. At the same time, a one-in-a-million shot from Cross popped the insurgent in the wrist.

CLACK–CLANK–CLACK!

The man's rifle skittered away down the corridor.

The injured man retreated back into the room. Before Chief Walker could close in on him, the Iraqi kicked the door shut.

SLAM! CLICK!

Then he locked it.

Cross, Walker, and Shepherd huddled together just outside the locked door. Walker and Shepherd glanced at Cross for orders. Cross took a position to the left of the door and motioned Walker to the opposite side. He signalled for Shepherd to get ready to kick the door in, but then gestured for him to hold position.

Cross tapped the small button on the two-way canal phone tucked into his right ear. "Fire Team Two, report," Cross said, whispering just loud enough for the tiny earbud radio to pick up his voice.

"All clear here, sir," Staff Sergeant Adam Paxton replied on the line. "The only man not accounted for is the one you went after."

"Good, we'll bring him round," Cross answered quietly. "Out." He paused for a moment to let the line clear, then tapped his canal phone again. "Overwatch, report."

"No rats, sir," Staff Sergeant Edgar Brighton reported. The USAF Combat Controller was stationed on the roof across the street with Lieutenant Kimiyo Yamashita, the team's sniper.

While Yamashita scanned the building and the street through the Leupold scope of his M110 sniper rifle, Brighton scanned the area through the high-resolution camera on his remote-controlled reconnaissance UAV quad-copter. "No sign of reinforcements, either."

"Good," Cross replied. "Out."

"Wait," Yamashita said. "Your fugitive is holed up in a room on the south face of the building, right?"

Cross took a moment to check his relative position in the building. "Affirmative," Cross said. "Do you have a visual on our target?"

"I can tell which room he went into, but I don't have a shot from this vantage point," Yamashita said. "I'm relocating now."

"Roger that," Cross said. "Out."

"Sir," Chief Walker said when comm-traffic in the team's canal phones stopped. He nodded at the closed door between them and the wounded Al Qaeda insurgent. "Let me try to talk to him. I can get him to come out."

Shepherd looked sceptical, but didn't say anything. Cross had his doubts too.

"He can't be more than eighteen years old, sir," Walker said, reading their expressions. "He's been shot twice already and he's probably scared to death. Let me give him a chance to surrender with his dignity intact. He'll take it."

Cross knew all about the chief's optimistic faith in humanity and how it occasionally clouded his judgement. However, Cross didn't like the idea of kicking in the door and gunning down a scared teenager any more than Walker did. So, with a nod, Cross motioned at the door. He kept his M4 ready, though, as did Shepherd.

"Son, I want you to listen to me," Walker spoke in Arabic, leaning against the door. "I know you're in pain, and I know you're losing blood. I know you're scared. But if you work with me, I can get you out of this mess without –"

"I have a way out!" the insurgent barked back.

The desperation in the boy's voice made Cross nervous, but at least it gave him a good sense of where he was standing. Cross exchanged a look with Shepherd, making sure the Green Beret would be ready to breach the door. Shepherd nodded.

"Let's talk about this," Walker said, his voice calm and steady, as if he were talking to one of his own kids back home. "What's your name?"

"Don't pretend you care who I am," the insurgent snarled in Arabic. "All you care about is –"

The boy's words stopped short as a muffled thump sounded from within the room. Cross thought he'd heard a sound like glass breaking but not shattering. After a moment, everything was silent. Cross didn't like that.

Cross signalled Shepherd to breach the door. Ignoring the frustration on Walker's face, Shepherd launched himself across the corridor.

CRUNCH!

He bashed the door off its hinges with a powerful kick. Cross and Walker were right on his heels as the three of them spread out to cover the room in all directions.

No sooner were they through the door when Yamashita's voice came over their canal phones. "Clear," the sniper said.

"Clear," Cross confirmed. Walker and Shepherd spread out to check the rooms on both sides. They both reported clear.

As Walker and Shepherd returned, Cross assessed the state of the room. Except for sturdy tables in each corner, the room had no furniture. A single window dominated the wall opposite the door. It had a small hole in it near the top, surrounded by a spiderweb of hairline cracks. The insurgent lay in the centre of the floor, sprawled on his face with his knees tucked under him. A dark stain was spreading out across the carpet beneath him.

To Cross's shock, the boy looked up at him. He was opening and closing his mouth as if he were trying to speak.

"He's alive!" Walker gasped. He tapped his canal phone as he crouched by the kid's side. "Medic! We need you up here now."

"On my way," Kyle Williams replied.

"Cancel that, Williams," Cross said. He met Chief Walker's wild, angry eyes with perfect calm.

"Sir," Williams said, signing off.

"He's not going to make it, Chief," Cross said. "There's nothing we can do for him now."

"Fine," Walker said. He glanced down and saw that the insurgent was already dead. "But Yamashita and I are going to have a talk later."

"Maybe you should put him in for a medal," Shepherd suggested in a low, respectful tone.

Walker glared angrily at Cross. Shepherd pointed below, then nudged the boy's outstretched right hand with the toe of his boot. Walker saw a gunmetal-grey device in the Iraqi's limp hand. Only then did Walker take a good look around the room to see what Cross and Shepherd had already noticed.

In all four corners of the room, on and under the tables, were stacked blocks of black market plastic explosives. One of the blocks on the table nearest the boy had an electronic detonator jammed into it. That one block alone would have killed everyone in the room. If all of them had gone off, the explosion would have easily levelled the building.

* * *

Several hours later, back at base, Shadow Squadron had squared away their gear and finished their After-Action Reports. As Cross entered the barracks, he saw that Chief Walker was giving Yamashita a piece of his mind regarding how the mission had ended.

"The kill wasn't necessary," Walker insisted. "I could've talked him down."

"I didn't know you were talking to him at all, Chief," Yamashita said. "I just saw him pick up that trigger and start waving it around."

As always, Yamashita was calm. Cross noted, however, that Walker was anything but composed. Even still, he waited and listened before intervening.

"What if it'd been a dead-man switch?" Walker demanded. "You would've brought that whole building down!"

Cross had to admit that was a good point. That kind of trigger would've been armed the moment the insurgent squeezed it, but wouldn't have gone off unless the insurgent let go.

"It wasn't a dead-man switch," Yamashita said.

"You could tell?" Cross asked.

"Sir," Yamashita replied with a nod. At the time, he'd been only about eighty per cent sure. But Yamashita decided that Walker and Cross didn't need to know that.

"He was hurt and scared, Lieutenant," Walker said, returning to his original point. "I could've got him to surrender. Nobody had to die. Especially not like that. I mean, you shot him in the throat."

Yamashita hadn't known that until now. "I was shooting through glass," Yamashita said, his voice calm and even. "I was aiming for his chest. Some deflection is unavoidable, even at that range."

"It was avoidable," Walker snapped. "You didn't have to take the shot! I mean, nobody ordered you to. If you hadn't jumped the gun, that boy would still be alive!"

Yamashita suppressed a shudder of rage. He started to say something, but Cross interrupted. "All right, Walker," Cross said. "You've made your position more than clear. It's time to let me handle this."

"Sir, I —" Walker began.

"Chief," Cross said, cutting him off. "I got it."

Walker was not satisfied, but he put up no further argument. He gave Yamashita one last cold look then stormed out of the room.

"Follow me, Lieutenant," Cross said. He led Yamashita to the room that served as his office while Shadow Squadron was stationed there.

Yamashita tried to put Chief Walker out of his mind. He understood where Walker was coming from, but the chief always believed he could save the world if he just tried hard enough. Walker had no idea what Yamashita had to deal with every time he pulled the trigger on his M110.

Cross sat down in the chair behind his wooden desk. He gestured for Yamashita to take the stool across from him. "Walker's pretty salty right now," Cross said. "Keep in mind that he's not angry at you. It's just the situation that bothers him."

Yamashita glanced through the open blinds on the window behind Cross. In the distance, he could see the massive Ziggurat of Ur that lay within the security perimeter of the air base. The ancient pile of bricks was over forty centuries old. It would still be there when the Iraqis and Americans were only a memory. "I know how Walker is," Yamashita finally said.

"Officially, you made the right call," Cross said. "I would have ordered you to take the shot. Next time, though, I need to know what you know. When you're on overwatch, you have to keep me informed of any new information you find."

Yamashita didn't reply, but some of what he was thinking must have shown on his face. Cross raised an eyebrow. "Something on your mind, Lieutenant?" Cross asked. "You can speak freely."

Yamashita hesitated. His previous Commanding Officer had said the exact same thing only to bait a trap. Cross didn't seem like the type, though. Yamashita decided to take the opportunity. "I know I should have told you as soon as I saw the C4 blocks on the tables," he said, looking at Cross's desk. "I was about to, but when that guy stuck the detonator in and picked up that trigger, I didn't think I had time. So I took the shot."

Cross narrowed his eyes. "That's fair," he said. "Just don't make a habit out of it."

Yamashita met Cross's eyes directly with his own. "Yes, sir," he said.

Cross nodded, satisfied with the response. "While I've got you here, is there anything else you need to talk about?" Cross asked. "I keep an open-door policy for my team."

"No, sir," Yamashita said immediately, even though it was a tempting offer. He stood and folded his hands behind his back. "If that's all . . ."

"Sure, you're dismissed," Cross said. He tapped his temple with his finger. "But if things start piling up in here, I need to know about it."

"Sir," Yamashita said. This time, Yamashita could see that Cross wasn't pleased by his one-word answer, but it was the best Yamashita could manage at the moment.

Yamashita lingered for a moment. Then he saluted and left.

INTEL

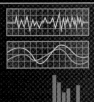

DECRYPTING
IIIIIIIIIII IIIIIIIIIIIIIIIIIIIIIIII

12345

COM CHATTER

- INFIDEL - "one without faith", or a non-believer

- RANGEFINDER - device that measures the distance from the observer to a target

- UAV - Unmanned Aerial Vehicle, or drone, used for covert surveillance

3245.98 ● ● ●

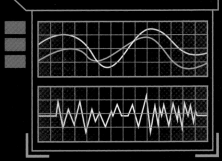

CHAPTER TWO

DIRTY VIP

1324.014

Within a week, Shadow Squadron had another local assignment. Cross called his team together in a conference room at Tallil Air Base. Staff Sergeant Brighton synced up a tablet computer with a palm-sized projector. It shone on the wall opposite the door.

The six squad soldiers sat around the conference table. Cross and Chief Walker stood at the front of the room on opposite sides of the projected computer display. For the moment, the screen displayed the swords-and-globe emblem of the Joint Special Operations Command.

"Morning," Cross said with a nod to the team. "We've got a situation developing with one of our human intelligence assets in Dhi Qar province. He's the same guy who's been feeding us all of our recent intel about insurgent activities. He believes he's been targeted for assassination, so he's asked us to supplement his private security force at a special event two days from now."

"He asked for us?" Yamashita asked, his eyes narrowed.

"He actually asked his CIA handler, Agent Bradley Upton," Chief Walker clarified. "Upton's Special Activities Division unit is stretched thin, so we've been asked to help them out."

"Since when do we do favours for the CIA?" Brighton asked.

Cross shrugged. "That's above my pay grade," he said. Yamashita thought the commander didn't look all too happy about this particular favour.

"So who's the asset?" Brighton asked.

"His name is Heshem Shadid," Cross replied.

Cross tapped on the tablet. An image of a middle-aged Iraqi man in an expensive suit popped up. He had a deep widow's peak of iron-grey hair. "Shadid is a recent addition to the Iraqi parliament in the Prime Minister's Islamic Dawa Party. Apparently, he's been with Al-Dawa since the Iran-Iraq War in the 1980s."

"Loyal," Brighton murmured, impressed. "The '80s and '90s weren't good times to be Al-Dawa."

In Yamashita's opinion, Brighton had missed the point. In the 1980s, during the Iran-Iraq war, Al-Dawa had been a terrorist organization devoted to promoting the Islamic religion. It had supported Iran's Islamic Revolution and received support from that country for efforts against the Baathists in Iraq. After a host of Al-Dawa terrorist activities, including the bombing of the US embassy in Kuwait in 1983, the Baathists had all but wiped out the remaining Al-Dawa members.

The few who survived the crackdown had either fled the country, or gone into hiding. It wasn't until the fall of Saddam Hussein's brutal regime that the

Baathists fell from power, which made it safe for Al-Dawa members to finally resurface.

Loyal or not, Al-Dawa had still committed terrorist acts against their own people. In Yamashita's opinion, they didn't deserve sympathy.

"In two days," Cross continued, "Shadid will be attending an exhibition football match at the An Nasiriyah Stadium. He's giving a speech before the match, hoping to earn popular support for his party."

"At least he'll have a captive audience," Brighton joked.

"That's enough, Sergeant," Walker growled, apparently fed up with Brighton's chatter. Yamashita was getting a little tired of it himself. He liked the Combat Controller, but the young soldier's lack of focus was sometimes distracting.

"Sorry, Chief," Brighton said.

Cross swiped the tablet's touch screen, bringing up a street map of Nasiriyah. One route blinked in red. "This is the route Shadid will follow from his place to the stadium, along with alternates. Agent

Upton's SAD unit will be on station at the house and at the stadium, co-ordinating with Shadid's personal security men. Our job is to secure the route and ride with Shadid. He'll be travelling in his armoured limo, and we've got our van. We'll use Brighton's UAV for aerial recon." He glanced at Yamashita and added. "We'll set you up midway for overwatch."

"Is there a specific threat against this guy?" the team's newest member, Second Lieutenant Aram Jannati, asked. Jannati had come out of the Marine Special Operations Regiment, replacing the deceased Neil Larssen. "Why do we believe he's been targeted for assassination?"

Cross swiped a few times on his tablet. "The day after his people issued the press release that said Shadid would be at An Nasiriyah Stadium, he received this picture in an unmarked envelope," the commander said.

Another photo of Shadid appeared. But this one had been altered. It showed Shadid getting out of his limo in front of the Baghdad Convention Centre, which was where the Parliament met. In the picture,

Shadid's left eye had been blacked out with a marker. The Arabic letters kāf, fā and rā had been drawn on his forehead.

Shepherd slowly frowned. "'Infidel,'" he said, interpreting the letters written on the picture. "That's not good."

"Infidel is *kafira*, with an alif," Chief Walker corrected. "This says *kefira*. It means 'disbelief'."

"On the back of the picture," Cross said, advancing to a new image on his tablet, "this word was written in marker." Printed neatly on the back of the photo in Arabic was the word *Zulfiqar*.

"Oh," Jannati said. "I see."

Yamashita didn't understand. Frowns on the rest of the men's faces told him that he was not alone.

Cross motioned for Jannati to explain. "Zulfiqar is the name of the Blade of Evil's Bane," Jannati said. "'*On the day of judgment, the Twelfth Imam will strike down the Deceiving Messiah.*' Zulfiqar is the sword he will use to kill him." He paused, then shrugged. "Or so the story goes, anyway."

Brighton rolled his eyes. "So our VIP is targeted for assassination by a guy using the name Zulfiqar," he said dryly.

Walker nodded. "Yes, it fits. According to the legends, that is how the Deceiving Messiah can be recognized. That, and the fact that he'll be trying to drive people away from an Islamic state."

"Do people think Shadid is doing that?" Jannati asked.

"Depends on who you ask," Cross said. "There are some who don't like the fact that Shadid and his party are disarming the militias. Some believe that disarming the militias is a step on the road back to a secular, or non-religious, state."

"That sounds like an excuse to fight for political power," Yamashita said with distaste in his voice.

"That's Agent Upton's read on it too," Cross answered. "From what Upton's people have gathered, this Zulfiqar business is just to put fear into Shadid's enemies. At its heart, though, this threat on Shadid's life is about nothing more than politics, power, and money."

"So it's just another sunny day in Iraq," Brighton said.

Some of the other men chuckled, but Yamashita didn't laugh. It wasn't funny – it was disgusting. His team was being asked to stand in harm's way, to potentially kill – people in order to protect a former terrorist and traitor. He'd joined the military because he wanted to protect America from its enemies, not to protect bad guys from *their* enemies.

Unfortunately, that turned out to be their job all too often. And Yamashita was getting sick of it.

* * *

Two hours after the briefing, Yamashita was dressed and ready for work. He sat in the passenger seat of a borrowed vehicle as Lieutenant Commander Cross drove all the main and back-up routes Shadid could possibly take to An Nasiriyah Stadium at week's end.

Every once in a while, Yamashita signalled to Cross to stop. Then he aimed out of the window with a high-tech laser rangefinding apparatus. He used the rangefinder to check lines of sight and measure

distances from the road to various firing positions that overlooked it. He'd already picked a few potential overwatch positions on the first trip from Shadid's front gate to the stadium. But Yamashita needed the fresh perspective of each trip to help him make up his mind. He also needed the extra time to try to reconsider his own perspective on the mission, as well as the life he'd chosen by joining Shadow Squadron.

Yamashita put down the rangefinder. The car got moving again. "What do you think?" Cross asked.

"The south-east corner room on the top floor of that building should do," Yamashita said, looking out of the window.

"That one?" Cross asked, leaning over briefly to look out of Yamashita's passenger-side window. "You sure?" He pointed to a taller building further away and said, "That one's taller. Looks like a better field of view over the back-up routes we might need to take through this part of town, too."

Yamashita met Cross's eyes and cocked an eyebrow. "With all due respect, Commander . . ."

Cross laughed. "All right, Lieutenant, I get it," he said. "You're the one with the sniper training. I'll trust your judgement."

"Sir," Yamashita said.

"You know, after I got my commission, I applied to sniper school," Cross said. "I didn't get in, though."

"No?" Yamashita said. "I've seen you shoot. What happened?"

"My CO at the time denied me," Cross said. "He wanted me fast-tracked for command, and he was worried that being a sniper would derail my career."

"He probably did you a favour," Yamashita said.

Cross looked straight at him, making Yamashita wish he'd held his tongue. "Why?" Cross asked.

Yamashita hesitated. "It suits some better than others," he said with a shrug.

"Oh?" Cross asked. "How does it suit you, Lieutenant?"

Yamashita frowned. He looked down at the rangefinder resting on his knees. He saw he was clenching the side of the device so hard that his knuckles were turning white. He forced himself to relax his grip.

After about a minute of silence, Cross finally pulled the vehicle they'd borrowed off the side of the road. He turned halfway around in his seat to look squarely at Yamashita. "Talk to me, Lieutenant," he said. "You've had a black cloud over your head since the mission briefing."

Yamashita knew that stubborn silence at a moment like this would only cause more problems in the long run. He took a breath to collect his thoughts. When he had finally found the same calm that he summoned whenever he pulled the trigger on his M110, he spoke. "I read Upton's report on Shadid after the meeting," he said. "He's a real piece of trash, our VIP. All these 'tips' he's been giving us on insurgents since we arrived are all his former associates. They are people he worked with when he was a terrorist. He sells them out to the CIA and we go and wipe them out. But if you look at it closely, a few years ago he was doing the kinds of things they are now."

Cross's face looked like he'd just tasted something unpleasant. He couldn't deny what Yamashita was saying, so he just nodded.

"So why should Shadid get a free ride when these other guys don't?" Yamashita said. "Why does he get to play politics with one hand while signing his old friends' death warrants with the other?"

"Because he's got what it takes to play the game," Cross said. "Shadid – and all the rest like him – were the first and loudest to step up and promise they could help us turn Iraq into a democracy. He's using his dark past to help us build a bright future for this country."

"His past is that he's a terrorist and a criminal," Yamashita said. His voice was as steady as his trigger finger. His thoughts, however, were anything but calm. "He doesn't care about the future. He just wants whatever power, money, and influence he can grab."

"True," Cross said with a sigh. "But where would this country be right now if not for opportunists like him? Think about the mission earlier this week. If not for intel Shadid provided, we'd never have known what that cell was planning. Think of the damage they could have done."

Yamashita knew Cross had a point, but it made the situation no easier to accept. "I know, I know, Commander," Yamashita said. "That's just the way things work here –"

"Not just here," Cross cut in. "This isn't any different from how lawyers back home make plea bargains with criminals to catch other, more dangerous criminals. As distasteful as it is, sometimes it's just better to let one scumbag go free if it gets a whole gang of scumbags off the street."

"I understand the logic, Commander," Yamashita said. "It makes me wonder whether we're actually doing long-term good, or just creating bigger problems for the next generation to deal with. Just like the last generation did for us."

"I wish I had the right answer, Lieutenant," Cross said. "But there just isn't one. The best we can do is focus on the small details about our jobs. That's all we have any control over."

"The small details," Yamashita repeated.

The sniper lapsed back into silence. He wasn't sure what he'd been expecting Cross to say, but "lock it down and walk it off" wasn't it. He was already trying to deal with things by focusing on the small scale. Doing his job – especially on overwatch – was all about focusing on the small scale. The flow of battle might change completely when he pulled the trigger, but it was easy to lose sight of that in the rifle scope. For him, combat occurred one bullet, one target, one shot at a time.

That was the heart of the problem now. Fate had let an evil man escape the punishment that Yamashita himself had doled out to that young Al Qaeda insurgent. The boy with the bomb. No matter what Walker said, that kid deserved to be taken out. Why, then, should Shadid get away with all the evil things he'd done?

If Shadid didn't deserve to live, Yamashita wondered, was he truly obliged to do everything he could to protect the man's life? He certainly wouldn't shoot Shadid himself.

But by *not* pulling the trigger – by not saving Shadid from those who wanted to kill him – maybe he could do the work that fate had apparently forgotten.

Maybe it was just that simple.

INTEL

DECRYPTING

12345

COM CHATTER

- AA-12 - box or drum-fed shotgun capable of fully automatic fire
- CANAL PHONE - an inside-the-ear style of headphone often used in military communications
- CORPSMAN - enlisted person in the US Army who works as a field medic

3245.98 ● ● ●

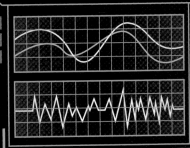

CHAPTER THREE

1324.014

SNIPER SHIELD

On the day of the football match and the politician's speech, Shadow Squadron travelled in the pre-dawn hours to Heshem Shadid's compound in Nasiriyah. It was a walled sandstone fortress that had escaped all damage from the fierce fighting in the US-led war. A pair of guards – one local man and one American SAD operative – met them at the gate. It took the guards about five minutes to clear them before their cars rolled inside.

Bradley Upton, the CIA agent who worked with Shadid, was there to greet them. Upton wore khakis and a button-down shirt with the sleeves rolled up to his elbows. He shook hands with each member of the Shadow Squadron team. Yamashita had no doubt that Upton was an experienced and competent field operative. However, his first impression of the man was that he looked like a middle-aged used car salesman. The agent's slick smile didn't do anything to dispel the image, either.

"Commander, I'm glad you could make it!" Upton said with too much enthusiasm. "The CIA appreciates the loan of your men and the use of your time."

"It wasn't my call," Cross answered. "Is there somewhere we can set up?"

"Right this way," Upton said, gesturing his arm with a flourish. If Upton took offence at Cross's comment, he didn't show it. "Shadid's waiting for us in the dining room."

Yamashita followed the team out of the foyer, then down a long corridor to a set of mahogany doors that led into Heshem Shadid's dining room. The long table down the centre was set for coffee, with trays of fruit at every seat. Heshem sat at one end of the table with the head of his security staff on his left. There was an empty chair on his right. When Upton entered the room, he headed for that chair. Shadid rose and met him halfway.

"Heshem," Upton said, "this is the rest of my security detail. They'll be handling your en-route security today."

Yamashita saw Cross scowl at Upton's description of his team. But the commander put on his professional demeanour and shook Shadid's hand with a smile.

"Mr Upton assures me your men are very talented," Shadid said to Cross in English. "We're looking forward to a safe journey."

Cross cocked his head at that. Upton's eyes narrowed just a little. "*We*, sir?" Cross asked. He looked at Upton. "Is there something we don't know?"

"A change of plans," Upton admitted. "Mister Shadid's ten-year-old grandson will be joining you today."

A faint electric charge seemed to move through the men of Shadow Squadron. All of them froze for a moment.

Cross glanced quickly from Upton to Shadid. "What's this?" he asked, his voice flat over suppressed annoyance. Yamashita had heard the commander use the same tone on Chief Walker plenty of times.

"Habib is a great fan of Younis Mahmoud, the captain of our national team," Shadid explained. "I promised him the chance to meet him after the game."

"That's fine," Cross said diplomatically. "But we should arrange to get him there separately."

"Nonsense," Shadid said, brushing the suggestion away with the back of his hand. "If you can keep me safe, you can keep us both safe."

"It's an unnecessary risk," Cross said.

"Quite the opposite," Shadid said. "I've made it known all week that Habib would be accompanying me to this engagement. By now, Zulfiqar's assassins undoubtedly have heard. From what I know of them from Mr Upton, I believe these men are not careless or barbaric. They won't risk taking Habib's life in an attempt to assassinate me."

"You can't be sure of that," Cross said through clenched teeth.

"I have the full faith that comes of my trust in your country," Shadid replied. Yamashita saw a flicker of a smug smile on the former terrorist's face. "I'm sure that having Habib with me will be the safest thing for both of us. Zulfiqar and his men might still make an attempt on *my* life. However, his honour will force them to take greater care not to harm any innocents. They will be bound by that honour, and that will make them easier for you to deal with."

"Did honour ever constrain you from harming innocents?" Yamashita muttered.

"You're referring to my . . . past?" Shadid said. He turned his cold eyes to Yamashita. "You can be certain, young man, that I am nothing like the man I used to be."

Yamashita looked up to find Cross, Chief Walker, and Agent Upton staring at him. Upton and Cross's

expressions were unreadable. Walker, however, was glaring at him with the same look of death he gave Brighton's dumb jokes.

Yamashita nodded at Shadid, then shut his mouth.

"Mr Upton and I have already talked about this," Shadid said to Cross. "Habib is coming with me. That ends the discussion."

"The customer's always right," Upton said, shrugging mock-apologetically to Cross.

"All right," Cross said. "It doesn't really change the plan, it just raises the stakes. So let's look at the routes."

At a signal from Cross, Brighton set up the palm projector on the table. The members of Shadow Squadron took up positions around the room. Cross broke out the tablet computer and began paging through the presentation he'd designed the day before. Upton had already signed off on it via email, and now Shadid nodded along with all the key points without arguing. He had got his way with regard to bringing his grandson along, so it seemed he was prepared to be flexible about everything else.

Listening quietly to the plan he'd already committed to memory, Yamashita couldn't take his mind off Shadid. He hadn't meant to say anything to the man, but the politician's gall and cowardice had surprised him. In Yamashita's mind, bringing a kid along in the hope of making criminal terrorists less likely to act was the height of complete stupidity. But the fact that Upton had agreed to it in the first place must have meant that Shadid was an intelligence asset of the utmost importance.

Even if Shadid was right about bringing his grandson along, what he was doing was no better than holding the boy up in front of himself as a human shield. That the man was willing to risk a child's life to protect his own only confirmed Yamashita's opinion of Shadid. For a moment, he was tempted to walk out of the room in protest. Or maybe "lose track" of Shadid en route to the event.

Yamashita's thoughts chased each other in his head as he half-listened to Cross's presentation. At the end, Upton brought the newcomers up to speed about what his unit would be doing and how they'd be co-ordinating with Shadid's small personal security force. Yamashita took mental notes, but none of that information affected his job, so he allowed himself to get lost in thought. He returned to full attention when Cross took control of the meeting again.

"Here's how we'll go," the commander said. He looked from Williams to Chief Walker. "Chief, you and the corpsman will ride in the limo with Shadid, Agent Upton, and the head of Mister Shadid's security."

"Sir," Walker and Williams said.

"You'll drive the van," Cross said to Staff Sergeant Paxton. Paxton nodded. Cross looked at Brighton next. "You'll be in the passenger seat and operate the UAV to keep us informed and connected."

"Sir," Brighton said, smiling proudly. A recent upgrade he'd made to his prized UAV, or Unmanned Aerial Vehicle, boosted the signal strength of the team's canal phone earbuds. The improvement allowed the soldiers to remain in clear contact at an even greater range. No doubt, he also liked the idea of being in the passenger seat. It gave him the chance to break out his baby – an AA-12 combat shotgun.

"I want you two in the back of the van," Cross said to Shepherd and Jannati. To Shepherd, he said, "You're in the hot seat." He looked at Jannati. "You're on ammo and support."

"Sir," the soldiers replied. Shepherd wore a huge grin. Jannati looked glum and disappointed. "Privilege of seniority, sir," Shepherd told the Marine. Although Jannati had more experience in the field, Shepherd had been with Shadow Squadron longer.

"And you're with me on overwatch," Cross said, finally addressing Yamashita. "We'll head out first and set up in the spot you picked yesterday." He looked at Walker. "When we're in position, I'll give you the go-ahead."

"Sir," Walker said.

"I'll get my teams in position," Upton said. "We'll go live on your signal, Commander."

"My men will take their orders from yours," Shadid said to Upton. He then opened his arms wide in a gesture that took in Cross and Upton and said, "I can't thank you both enough for this."

"We're just doing our jobs, Shadid," Upton said.

"Gear up and get ready to move out," Cross said to his team, ignoring Shadid entirely. He looked at Yamashita and said, "Lieutenant, you're with me."

"Sir," Yamashita replied. He turned and followed Cross out. On the way, he stole one last glance at Heshem Shadid.

INTEL

DECRYPTING

12345

COM CHATTER

- CONVOY - a group of vehicles travelling together for protection
- KHAYBAR - Iranian-designed assault rifle capable of full-auto fire
- IED - improvised explosive device, or a homemade roadside bomb
- RPG - rocket-propelled grenade, or a shoulder-fired, anti-tank weapon

3245.98 ● ● ●

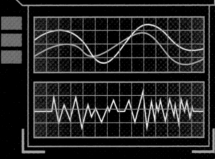

CHAPTER FOUR

JUDGEMENT

1324.014

The sun was just coming up when Cross and Yamashita took their places in the overwatch position. They built a sniper nest in the corner room of an empty seven-story building. The structure had taken a great deal of damage during the Battle of Nasiriyah. The room they'd chosen was missing its roof and part of the wall at the corner, which gave them a commanding view of the route below as well as the buildings across the street. It also offered cover from any firing position from seven stories and below.

Yamashita assembled his M110 sniper rifle while Cross hung a sheet of sand-coloured netting across the widest gaps in the broken wall. The material was so sheer that Yamashita could aim and shoot through it from up close. At the same time, anyone who might be inclined to fire back wouldn't be able to see him from more than a few metres away.

When the net was in place, Yamashita lay down just behind it on top of a cushion. His rifle barrel rested only a few millimetres from the netting. Cross sat a couple of metres away with a tablet computer on his lap. The tablet was synced to Brighton's UAV, providing a live feed from the drone's camera.

After a quick comm-check and an all-ready report from Chief Walker, Cross set the operation in motion.

While they waited for the van and Shadid's limo to come into view, Yamashita said, "You've never taken overwatch before, Commander."

"True," Cross said. "But Chief Walker made the point last night that putting myself on the front lines for every mission isn't exactly wise. So I'm trying this out." He hesitated then added, "Plus, I wasn't sure I could trust myself to behave if I had to ride in the limo with our VIP and Upton."

"Fair enough," Yamashita said.

It wasn't until an hour later that Shadid and his grandson were ready to go. It took another fifteen minutes for the limo and Shadow Squadron's nondescript black van to get moving. Brighton kept the UAV high and centred, allowing Cross a good view of the route and the surrounding side streets. Traffic here wasn't as bad as it was in central Nasiriyah, but Cross still had to direct the team around several accidents.

Four of Shadid's personal security guards rode in front of his limo on motorcycles, trying to ease the way through traffic. As they approached an intersection, two of the motorcycles pulled ahead and blocked the side streets so the limo's way would be clear. Then, while those two waited, the other pair of riders moved ahead to the next intersection. When intersections were close together, it made for a lot of stops and long pauses – and a lot of unhappy morning commuters.

The small convoy came into view of the sniper's perch at last. At this point, they were half an hour behind schedule. "Got a visual," Yamashita murmured to Cross.

"So far so good," Cross said, his eyes glued to the tablet's screen. "You see anything?"

"It's clear," Yamashita said.

Below, the VIP's procession made a turn onto a side street with no cars on it. That street was the longest, straightest part of the route, offering overwatch the best field of view. The van and limo rolled down practically by themselves as the motorcycles leapfrogged ahead of them.

"Um, something's wrong here," Brighton's voice reported over the team's canal phones. "You see it too, Commander?"

"Yeah," Cross said with a tap on his earbud. "It's awfully quiet here. Where is everybody? I don't like this. Chief, tell your driver –"

A huge ball of dust and smoke blossomed on the street below, interrupting Cross. A second later came the boom and rattle of an explosion.

A roadside bomb detonated in a rubbish bin at the intersection just behind the team's van. It did no damage to the vehicles, but the security man on the rear motorcycle disappeared in the fire and smoke. Another rider was knocked off his bike.

"IED!" Brighton shouted. "Where the –"

BANG!

A second explosion went off across the street a little further ahead, unseating the forward rider on that side.

"Chief, report!" Cross barked.

"We're secure!" Chief Walker yelled over the canal phones. "Where is – hey, slow down, you maniac!"

The driver of Shadid's limo panicked and stepped on the accelerator. Wheels spun and smoked as the vehicle skidded away.

"Stay on them!" Cross ordered.

"Sir," Paxton replied. He gunned the van's engine and took off after the fleeing limo.

"Yamashita, two blocks up," Cross said.

Two blocks ahead of the limo, a car came barrelling down an alley on an intercept course. "Got it," Yamashita said. He took aim on the windshield for a closer look. "It's empty, sir."

Yamashita shifted his aim.

FWIP!

He squeezed off a round into the car's engine block. A burst of flame and a plume of black smoke billowed from under the hood, but the shot came too late. Before the limo driver even saw it, the burning car launched out of the alley and hit the limo in the rear driver-side fender.

CRASH!

The limo swerved, bounced onto the curb, and then rammed into the corner of a building.

Yamashita took a moment to scan up the alley where the car had come from. He saw a single figure at the far end – presumably the man who'd set the car in motion. He was running down the alley with a rifle in his hands. Yamashita pulled the trigger.

FWIP!

The man collapsed.

"RPG!" Cross and Brighton called out at once.

"On top of the warehouse!" Cross added.

Yamashita swivelled his rifle at the rooftop of the building across the street from where the limo had crashed. The first thing he saw was the open door on the roof-access stairway swinging closed. A second later, he saw a man in a black hood leaning over the edge of the roof with a rocket-propelled grenade launcher.

FWIP!

Yamashita and the masked man fired at the same time. The man on the roof toppled headlong off the warehouse, but not before his RPG streaked a line of white smoke through the air.

KA-BOOOOOOOM!

The grenade hit the pavement just behind the limo's front-passenger tyre. The car bucked and slammed down, thick smoke pouring out of its front end.

"Sergeant, get up here!" Walker yelled to Paxton over the canal phone. When the chief transmitted, Yamashita could hear someone coughing. Then he heard Shadid's terrified grandson crying hysterically. It sent a primal shiver down Yamashita's spine to hear the boy howl. To force a child into this situation made the politician the lowest of the low.

"We're here," Paxton said. He whipped his van around the damaged limo.

SKREEEEEEEE!

They stopped just ahead of the vehicle in the street.

"Chief, damage report," Cross said.

"Driver's dead," Walker responded. "Ursa Major has a broken leg; Ursa Minor is unhurt. Mister Know-It-All is unconscious."

"Hang tight," Cross said. He looked at Yamashita. "Do you see anybody else?"

With a long, steady sweep, Yamashita scanned the street for attackers. Then he traced a line up the side of a building overlooking the street from the opposite end of the area. Last, he turned his attention back to the scene unfolding around the van. "Streets are clear, sir," Yamashita said.

"Sir?" Walker called, his voice tense.

"All right, Chief," Cross replied. "Get the VIPs and Mister Know-It-All in the van. Ursa Minor first."

"Sir," Walker replied.

"I'll get the doors," Jannati said.

"I'm going to need some help with these other two," Williams said.

"I got it," Brighton replied.

Brighton hopped out of the passenger-side door of the van with his AA-12 combat shotgun. He ran back to the limo as Second Lieutenant Jannati popped the van's back door open. Meanwhile, Chief Walker was half-climbing, half-falling out of the back passenger door of the limo with his M4 carbine in one hand and the wildly struggling Habib Shadid under his other arm.

"Whoa!" Cross shouted over the canalphone. "Cover! TAKE COVER!"

Through his scope, Yamashita saw the metal door on the loading bay of a nearby warehouse roll up to reveal a team of gunmen behind a makeshift barricade of oil drums and sandbags. The man in the middle of the team stood behind a tripod-mounted machine gun.

As soon as the door cleared his firing line, the machine gunner took aim. Yamashita sighted on him at the same time. FWIP! One shot to the chest put him down. As he fell, the gunner squeezed the trigger convulsively.

RAT-TAT-TAT-TAT!

Bullets sprayed out wildly. Careless impacts traced a line across the street between the limo and the van, just missing Brighton as he crossed through the gap. He dived back and shoulder-rolled to safety behind the van's open back door as Walker pulled Shadid's terrified grandson behind the open door of the limo.

In the warehouse, another of the gunmen pushed the dead man out of the way of the machine gun. Unfortunately, he stayed out of Yamashita's sights by ducking low as he sprayed bullets without looking.

The shots chewed into the armour plating on the side of the van and broke up the road a bit, but did no serious damage. His fellows behind the barricade opened up with bullpup Khaybar rifles, pinning the Shadow Squadron soldiers inside or behind the vehicles.

"Covering fire!" Walker called out.

"Yamashita?" Cross asked.

"No shot, sir," the sniper said. He didn't have a clear line of sight to the gunmen to do more than waste a bullet on a minor wound. If the man spraying the MG3 would stop firing for just a second, Yamashita might be able to shoot it and take it out of commission. But that wasn't an option at the moment.

"All right," Cross said. He tapped his canal phone. "Hot seat, you're up."

"Yes, sir!" Shepherd said, sounding far too excited at the prospect of battle.

Brighton took a deep breath, then said, "I'm on it, sir," He hefted his AA-12 shotgun and whipped around the corner of the van screaming an inarticulate battle cry.

Yamashita saw a couple of the shooters pop up behind their Khaybars in surprise. He could have taken one or two of them down, but he knew Brighton had things under control.

Brighton cleared his cover and opened fire with his combat shotgun on full auto.

BOOM!

    BOOM!

  BOOM!

      BOOM!

        BOOM!

    BOOM!

The weapon roared like a lion as Brighton let fly. With a fire rate of 300 rounds per minute and a 12-gauge bore, the AA-12 filled the air with lead. One of the gunmen fell lifeless to the ground. Several shots punched into the barricade so hard that sand flew out like firework sparks.

Satisfied, Brighton dashed over to Walker's cover behind the limo's armoured door and knelt down next to him. "Drum!" Brighton shouted, ejecting the shotgun's spent ammo drum. Jannati threw him a second one from the back of the van. Brighton rammed it home and leant around the edge of the limo. He saw one of the gunmen peeking out from behind cover to try his luck again. Instead of aiming at the gunmen, Brighton lined up his sight with their machine gun and let loose.

BANG!

BANG!

KA-RANG!

The blasts knocked the weapon off its tripod.

"I'll take it from here," Shepherd said over the comm-channel.

Before the gunmen in the warehouse could peek out again, a circular hatch in the roof of the van popped open. Sergeant Shepherd rose through the opening behind a mounted M134 mini-gun. His back was to Yamashita, but the sniper was willing to bet that Shepherd was smiling from ear to ear.

"Light 'em up, Sergeant," Cross said, his voice cold and quiet.

"Hoo-rah!" Shepherd said.

WHIR-WHIR-
WHIR-WHIR-
WHIR-WHIR

Yamashita couldn't look away as Shepherd hit the firing button on the M134. Its six Gatling-style barrels spun up and put out a laser-accurate stream of 7.62x51mm NATO rounds at a rate just shy of 50 rounds per second. Whirring like a chainsaw, the mini-gun sprayed its ammo like a power hose spraying water.

Shepherd swept an arc of fire across the kill zone, then back again. Bullets tore through the barricade

like it was made of wet paper, annihilating the men behind it. None of them even had a chance to return fire before they were cut down.

A moment later, Shepherd let up to see if anyone returned fire or tried to run away. No one moved. "Clear," Shepherd said.

"Roger that," Cross replied. "Chief, get the VIPs out of the limo and in the van before anybody else shows up."

"Sir," Walker said. Once more he began carrying Habib Shadid over toward the van. The boy had stopped struggling, but from the glimpse Yamashita caught of his face, it was because he was in shock.

When Walker was clear, Brighton ducked into the back of the limo. He emerged a moment later with Heshem Shadid. Williams was right behind the politician, gently pushing the older man along.

Yamashita began to scan the horizon, silently enjoying the look of pain he'd seen on Heshem Shadid's face. That's when Yamashita saw it: under cover of a rooftop ledge, a sniper was taking aim at something down below. Yamashita didn't have a clear shot from his position, but there was no mistaking the prone position and the gun barrel.

What happened next occurred in the span of a second, but to Yamashita's whirling thoughts it lasted much longer. Part of him wanted to watch and do nothing. He relished the thought of Heshem Shadid's final moments in this world filled with intense pain and fear.

Yet as that savage thrill flickered inside him, disgust rose up and overwhelmed it. Was this who he was now, the sniper wondered? If Neil Larssen were still alive, would he be able to look his friend in the eye after what he was about to let happen?

After this, would he be able to look at himself in the mirror? Would he ever see himself the same way, or would he always see his reflection glaring back with silent anger?

"No," Yamashita said. "No!" He tapped his canal phone. "Brighton, get down! Sniper!"

Without a word, Brighton whipped the wobbling Shadid back around in a half circle and shoved him back over to Williams. At that precise instant, a bullet meant for Shadid's heart whizzed between his head and Brighton's.

KARANNNNNNNG!

The shot bounced off the armoured roof of the limo. Williams pulled Shadid into the limo, then Brighton jumped in after him and slammed the door.

"Where is he?" Cross demanded. He had Yamashita's rangefinder binoculars before his eyes, frantically scanning rooftops.

"He's in my sights," Yamashita said. He set his crosshairs on the muzzle flare as the sharpshooter – who could be none other than Zulfiqar himself — took his second shot.

CRACK!

The projectile lodged in the bulletproof window. "A little help here!" Brighton yelled over the comm-channel.

Yamashita didn't give Zulfiqar another chance to fire.

CLICK!

About half a kilometre away, the silhouette of the enemy sniper jerked once, then slumped over sideways. The barrel of his rifle lifted up like a flag pole.

For a moment, silence reigned, with nothing moving in that distant space.

Calm as ever came Yamashita's voice:

"Clear."

INTEL

DECRYPTING
|||||||||| ||||||||||||||||||

12345

COM CHATTER

- DEBRIEFING - the process of getting
information from a soldier after a
mission is over

3245.98 ● ● ●

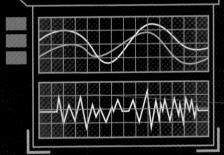

CHAPTER FIVE

A SOLDIER

1324.014

Several hours later – once Shadid, his grandson, and Agent Upton were all safe in the van with the rest of the Shadow Squadron – Cross and Yamashita stood together over Zulfiqar's body. Two motorcycles they'd borrowed from Shadid's fallen bodyguards stood waiting for them downstairs.

Across the room, Zulfiqar's rifle – a variant of the Russian Dragunov sniper rifle – was still propped up where the man's fall had pinned it.

Cross pulled the rifle away from the dead man and ejected the 10-round box magazine onto the floor. "I told you we should've picked this place," he said, glancing out the window. "Best sniper perch in the area."

Yamashita leant against the door frame to keep an eye out down the corridor. "I didn't want the best spot," the sniper said. "I wanted the second best perch."

"Sure you did, Lieutenant," Cross said with a smirk. "Because you knew Zulfiqar would want the best sniper spot for himself? And you knew he'd just be waiting up there for his men to flush Shadid out of cover so he could take him out? Is that what you're trying to say?"

"I'm no mind reader, Commander," Yamashita said. "But this is the spot I would have chosen if I had wanted to kill Shadid."

"True," Cross said. "If you were Zulfiqar, you mean."

Cross left the man's body where it lay and crossed the room to face Yamashita. The sniper met Cross's eyes warily.

"Then again," Cross said, "you're not Zulfiqar – you're you. If you had wanted Shadid dead, all you would've needed to do was hesitate at just the right moment . . . and watch as Zulfiqar took his shot."

Yamashita paused for a moment. Then he said, "If that's the kind of solider I was, then you'd have to keep me at arm's length during every mission. You'd have to be breathing down my neck at all times – looking over my shoulder to make sure I did the right thing."

"No," Cross said. His smirk and sarcastic tone were gone. In its place was an intensely serious, searching gaze that burned into Yamashita's eyes. "If you were that kind of soldier, you'd be off my team so fast it would make your head spin."

"Then I'm glad I'm not that type of soldier, Commander," Yamashita said.

As the words came out, Yamashita knew they were true. He'd flirted with temptation, and had almost given in. But the regret he would have felt for the rest of his life stayed his hand. Or rather, helped him pull the trigger.

"Good," Cross said, patting the sharpshooter on the back. "Let's keep it that way."

"Sir," Yamashita said, the hint of a smile on his face.

LOADING...

2012.101

MISSION DEBRIEFING

OPERATION

SNIPER SHIELD 1234

PRIMARY OBJECTIVES

- Meet with the VIP and his personal security force

- Prep a route and determine an overwatch position for transit

- Protect the VIP en route to his destination

STATUS

3/5 COMPLETE

SECONDARY OBJECTIVES

x Avoid open conflict with Iraqi insurgents

x Keep our presence covert

3245.98 ● ● ●

YAMASHITA, KIMIYO

RANK: Lieutenant
BRANCH: Army Ranger
PSYCH PROFILE: The team's sniper is an expert marksman and a true stoic. It seems his emotions are as steady as his trigger finger.

Operation Sniper Shield was a perfect example of a worst-case scenario. Everything went wrong, the assigned tasks were complex and varied, and there was a fair amount of dislike for the VIP we were assigned to protect. But from the outside looking in, no one could have known it; our men performed with remarkable proficiency and courage, despite any reservations.

As for me, I can't say it was easy to safeguard the life of an evil man. But if I wanted *easy*, I wouldn't have chosen to become a sniper — or join Shadow Squadron.

— Lieutenant Kimiyo Yamashita

2019.581

CARL BOWEN

Carl Bowen is a father, husband, and writer living in Georgia, USA. He was born in the state of Louisiana, lived briefly in England, and was raised in Georgia, where he went to school. He has published novels, short stories, and comics, and has retold the classic tales *20,000 Leagues Under the Sea*, *The Strange Case of Dr Jekyll and Mr Hyde*, *The Jungle Book*, *Aladdin and the Magic Lamp*, *Julius Caesar*, and *The Murders in the Rue Morgue*. He is the original author of *BMX Breakthrough* as well as the Shadow Squadron series.

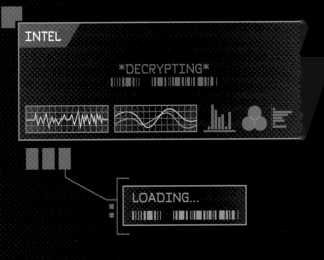

INTEL

DECRYPTING

LOADING...

ARTIST

WILSON TORTOSA

Wilson "Wunan" Tortosa is a Filipino comic book artist best known for his works on *Tomb Raider* and the American relaunch of *Battle of the Planets* for Top Cow Productions. Wilson attended Philippine Cultural High School, then went on to the University of Santo Tomas, where he graduated with a Bachelor's Degree in Fine Arts, majoring in Advertising.

COLOURIST

BENNY FUENTES

Benny Fuentes lives in Villahermosa, Tabasco, in Mexico, where the temperature is just as hot as the sauce. He studied graphic design in college, but now he works as a full-time colourist in the comic book and graphic novel industry for companies such as Marvel, DC Comics, and Top Cow Productions. He shares his home with two crazy cats, Chelo and Kitty, who act like they own the place.

2019.681

AUTHOR DEBRIEFING

ACCESS GRANTED

CARL BOWEN

Q/When and why did you decide to become a writer?
A/I've enjoyed writing ever since I was in elementary school. I wrote as much as I could, hoping to become the next Lloyd Alexander or Stephen King, but I didn't sell my first story until I was in college. It had been a long wait, but the day I saw my story in print was one of the best days of my life.

Q/What made you decide to write Shadow Squadron?
A/As a kid, my heroes were always brave knights or noble loners who fought because it was their duty, not for fame or glory. I think the special ops soldiers of the US military embody those ideals. Their jobs are difficult and often thankless, so I wanted to show how cool their jobs are, but also express my gratitude for our brave warriors.

Q/What inspires you to write?
A/My biggest inspiration is my family. My wife's love and support lifts me up when this job seems too hard to keep going. My son is another big inspiration.

He's three years old, and I want him to read my books and feel the same way I did when I read my favourite books as a kid. And if he happens to grow up to become an elite soldier in the US military, that would be pretty awesome, too.

Q/Describe what it was like to write these books.
A/The only military experience I have is a year I spent in the Army ROTC. It gave me a great respect for the military and its soldiers, but I quickly realized I would have made a pretty awful soldier. I recently got to test out a friend's arsenal of firearms, including a combat shotgun, an AR-15 rifle, and a Barrett M8Z sniper rifle. We got to blow apart an old fax machine.

Q/What is your favourite book, movie, and game?
A/My favourite book of all time is *Don Quixote*. It's crazy and it makes me laugh. My favourite movie is either *Casablanca* or *Double Indemnity*, old black-and-white movies made before I was born. My favourite game, hands down, is *Skyrim*, in which you play a heroic dragonslayer. But not even *Skyrim* can keep me from writing more Shadow Squadron stories, so you won't have to wait long to read more about Ryan Cross and his team. That's a promise.

2019.681

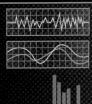

COM CHATTER

- MISSION PREVIEW: SEA DEMON
A contingent of well-organized Somali pirates have kidnapped several civilians at sea, including a VIP from the World Food Programme. The pirates, self-identified as Sea Demons, are holding the hostages for millions of dollars in ransom. None of the governments involved are willing to provide the funds.

3245.98 ● ● ●

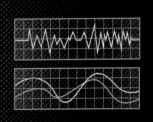

1324.014

SEA DEMON

Ever so slowly, Cross and Walker crawled on their bellies across the exposed ground towards the pirates' compound. The wet, tropical heat was nearly unbearable. Insects Cross had never even heard of treated them like a buffet table. Within minutes, the two men were covered with itching bites. But all they could do was ignore the discomfort. Any sudden or quick movements could result in a barrage of automatic rifle fire. The name of the game was patience.

After what seemed like an eternity, Walker and Cross had crawled to about ten metres of the patrolling sentries without any alarm going off. The sentries looked at ease and relaxed. They had no idea what was coming.

With a twitch of his finger, Cross signalled for Walker to halt. Behind them, Williams, Brighton, Shepherd, and Larssen all stopped as well. As the unaware sentries chatted with each other in Somali, Cross tightened his grip on his black tactical knife. Walker readied a well-used but razor-sharp KA-BAR blade that was older than he was. When the sentries passed, Cross tapped his canal phone twice, signalling Yamashita.

Then Cross popped up behind the sentries from his prone position. Walker sprang to his feet at the same time. Lightning quick, the two of them pounced on the sentries. Cross and Walker dragged their targets down, then silenced them with their blades.

Quietly, carefully, Walker and Cross dragged their targets out of sight. At the same moment, Lieutenant Yamashita squeezed off a single round from his M110 sniper rifle. The weapon's suppressor hid the muzzle flare and reduced the sound of the shot to nothing more than a cough. On the watchtower, the lookout sat down hard in the corner, then slumped over on his side.

"Tower clear," came Yamashita's voice through Cross's earpiece.

"Perimeter clear," Cross breathed, barely loud enough for the canal phone to register. "Confirm?"

"Confirmed," Paxton, Yamashita's spotter, replied. "And no additional sentries spotted. No one from the compound appears to be aware of our presence."

Cross and Walker nodded to each other as they cleaned their blades on the backs of the sentries' jackets. They returned their knives to their sheaths, and then produced their suppressor-equipped M4 carbine rifles.

Williams, Brighton, Shepherd, and Larssen split up into their respective fire teams. With the sentries neutralized, they wouldn't need to low-crawl anymore. But they stayed low and stepped as lightly as they could. No sense in riling up the pirates prematurely.

With Williams in tow, Cross retraced the sentries' path. They moved parallel to the length of the pirate compound until the guards on the longhouse were cut off from sight. Meanwhile, Walker led Brighton, Shepherd, and Larssen in the opposite direction. They took up strategic positions around the pirates' mess and barracks. As the four of them got ready, Cross and Williams made their way around the darkened rear of the longhouse. They crept through the shadows towards the two men guarding the hostages. Cross moved inside first, keeping Williams hidden in the darkness.

Cross tapped his canal phone. "Ready, Commander," Yamashita replied in the earpiece.

Cross took a deep breath to swallow down the excitement. He took a second breath. Then a third. Centring himself, Cross crept up to the corner of the longhouse and tapped his earphone twice more to give Yamashita the signal. A split second later, a pinpoint-accurate shot from Yamashita's rifle took out the outdoor light mounted on the face of the longhouse.

None of the pirates heard the shot itself, but the sound of the light fixture shattering into a million pieces definitely caught their attention. A second and third shot in quick succession took out the lights over the mess and barracks. The guards bolted up from their chairs waving their AK-47s back and forth wildly, trying to locate the threat. Other pirates nearby scrambled into frantic activity.

As pieces from the shattered lights rained down, Cross was already coming around the corner. One of the longhouse guards had his back to Cross.

A three-round burst from Cross's silenced carbine struck the pirate between his shoulder blades. The man fell dead into the arms of his compatriot. Their weapons were trapped between them for a crucial, fatal instant.

The second guard had heard the first set of muffled shots, but hadn't realized what was happening before his partner had collapsed. Cross opened fire with a second burst. The bullets caught him in the chest and dropped him lifeless to the ground. Neither man had so much as cocked his weapon.

Their deaths, however, hadn't gone unnoticed. The eight guards who remained at sea level saw the lights blow out, followed by a fully armed man darting into their midst from the darkness. Although caught off guard by the suddenness of the attack, they were at least trained well enough to react like soldiers rather than frightened rats. None of them had their AK-47s in hand, but several of them carried pistols strapped to their hips. Several pirates drew and raised them to open fire.

Bullets whizzed through the air, digging into the ground and splintering the wall of the longhouse all around Cross. But Cross hadn't stopped moving. He launched around a corner and dived for cover around the far side of the building. He rolled into a patch of fresh shadow, but the startled pirates quickly closed in on his position.

Their quick and well-trained reactions, however, just put the pirates in more danger. They hadn't realized they were dealing with more than one man. As they advanced on Cross's position with weapons raised, Walker and his three-man fireteam opened fire.

From the darkness, Brighton, Walker, and Larssen cut down the two pirates closest to Cross with precise shots. As they stepped into the light from behind the shadows of the barracks, the soldiers came face to face with two unarmed pirates looking for cover. At the sight of Brighton's masked face and the barrel of his AA-12 combat shotgun, the pirates skidded gracelessly to a stop, then stumbled in the opposite direction. Brighton grinned. He hadn't even needed to pull the trigger – they were headed right where he wanted them.

At the same moment, Staff Sergeant Shepherd rose from a prone position ten or so metres away. Shepherd's bipod-mounted M240L machine gun had nothing to suppress the sound or flash as he opened fire.

The automatic weapon's roar frightened even the bravest of the pirates. Lucky for them, Shepherd didn't target any of the pirates specifically. He was using the thundering machine gun fire in order to corral them into the mess hall . . .

TRANSMISSION ERROR

PLEASE CONTACT YOUR LOCAL LIBRARY
OR BOOKSHOP FOR MORE INFORMATION...

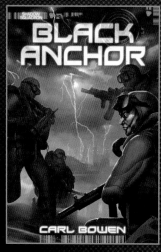

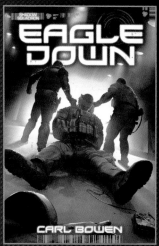

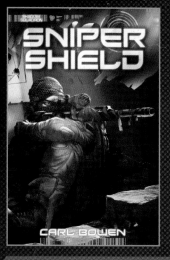

2012.101